the Cheetah Girls 2

cheetah chatter:

A Dictionary of Growl-licious Lingo

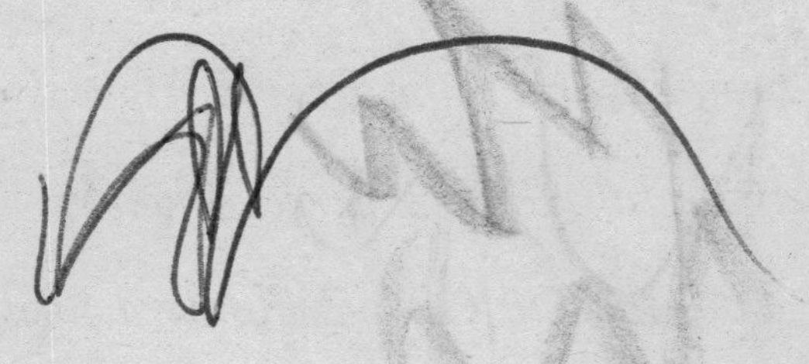

these books are Cheetah-licious!

The Cheetah Girls
Original Movie Junior Novelization

The Cheetah Girls Quiz Book

The Cheetah Girls Supa-Star Scrapbook

The Cheetah Girls 2 Junior Novel

XOXO The Cheetah Girls 2 Postcard Book

cheetah chatter:

A Dictionary of Growl-licious Lingo

From The Cheetah Girls book series

by Deborah Gregory

New York

Text by Emma Harrison

For more information address Disney Press, 114 Fifth Avenue, New York, New York 10011-5690.

Printed in the United States of America
First Edition
3 5 7 9 10 8 6 4

Library of Congress Catalog Card Number on file.
ISBN 0-7868-4716-6

You are a cheetah-licious divette and you want everyone around you to know it, am I right? Well, to truly show your superspecial spots, you have to be down with a certain lingo. If someone tells you that you're gonna "blow up big-time," you've got to know if that's a compliment or a diss. If you don't know, you're going to *look* like you don't know, you know? And no one wants that.

So the Cheetah Girls have put together a little book of words we use—words that show we have that extra-special sass. Read on, and soon you'll be growling like a true Cheetah!

XOXO

Galleria

all about

to be totally focused on something or someone

✓ **Do say:** The Cheetah Girls are **all about** winning the New Voices competition.

✗ **Don't say:** I am **all about** chowing down on today's cafeteria mystery meat.

attitude

A cool, confident vibe that a person projects. Of course, some people can have *too much* attitude.

✓ **Do say:** Galleria knows how to work that **attitude**.

✗ **Don't say:** Mom! I am so sick of your **attitude**!

backup

Singers who accompany a lead vocalist. They usually flesh out harmonies and support the lead voice.

✓ **Do say:** Dorinda and Aqua joined the Cheetah Girls as **backup**, but they have become so much more!

✗ **Don't say:** You guys have no say in what we do. You're just **backup**.

More than; extremely. Use this word when you really want to make your point.

✓ **Do say:** That Derek is **beyond** hot!

✗ **Don't say:** That dentist was **beyond** fun!

big time

that high point on the ladder of success when you can truly call yourself a celebrity

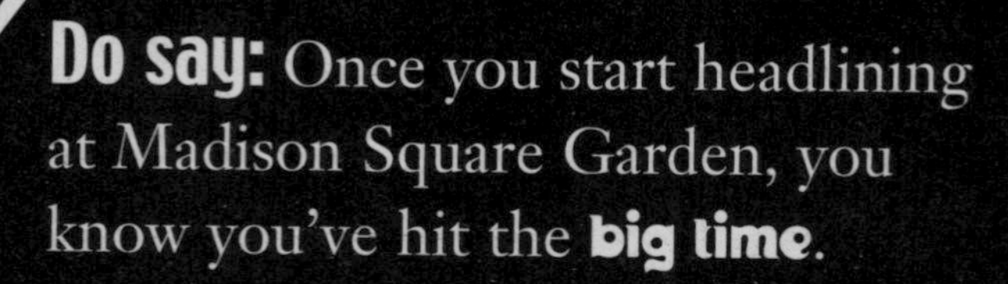

✓ **Do say:** Once you start headlining at Madison Square Garden, you know you've hit the **big time**.

✗ **Don't say:** We're performing at Pucci's birthday party? Girls, we've hit the **big time**.

blast

to insult someone
or something

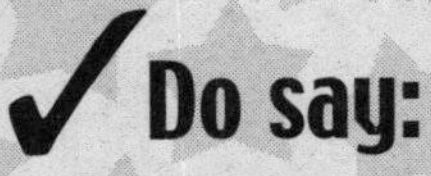

Do say:

Don't be **blasting** Aqua's hot sauce. She'll take it personally!

✗ Don't say:

I like to **blast** the Cheetah Girls' new album.

The fabulous gold, jewels, and other fine stuff that stars sport on the red carpet. (There used to be only two *bling*s, but we Cheetahs are always shooting for more.)

✓ **Do say:** Once our record hits number one and we make our millions, we are gonna be covered in **bling bling bling!**

✗ **Don't say:** **Bling bling bling?** (Yawn) Bo-ring.

blow up big-time

to get hugely famous in a super-short time

✓ **Do say:** When the Cheetah Girls' first single hits the airwaves, they are gonna **blow up big-time**!

✗ **Don't say:** If I eat one more bite, I'm gonna **blow up big-time**.

boo

special someone

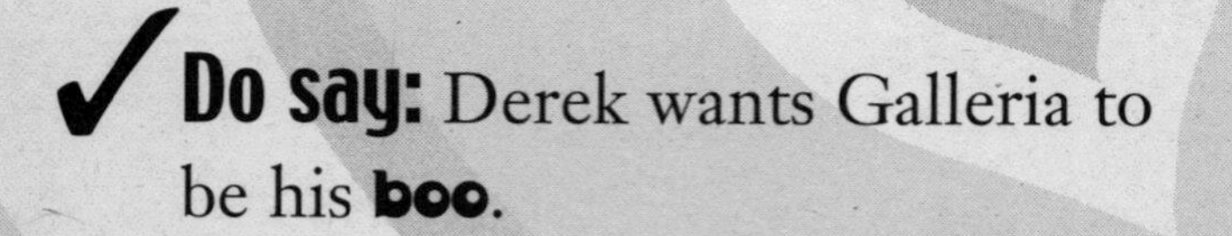

✓ **Do say:** Derek wants Galleria to be his **boo**.

✗ **Don't say:** Where's my little **boo**-boo? I just wuv my little **boo**!

tell me the nitty-gritty truth

✓ **Do say:** Just **bottom-line me**. What's it really going to take to get the Cheetah Girls to the top?

✗ **Don't say:** **Bottom-line me**, what's really in the cafeteria chili? (You don't want to know!)

to leave

✓ **Do say:** This party stinks. Let's **bounce**.

✗ **Don't say:** Your folks bought a new trampoline? Let's **bounce**!

bug out

go crazy

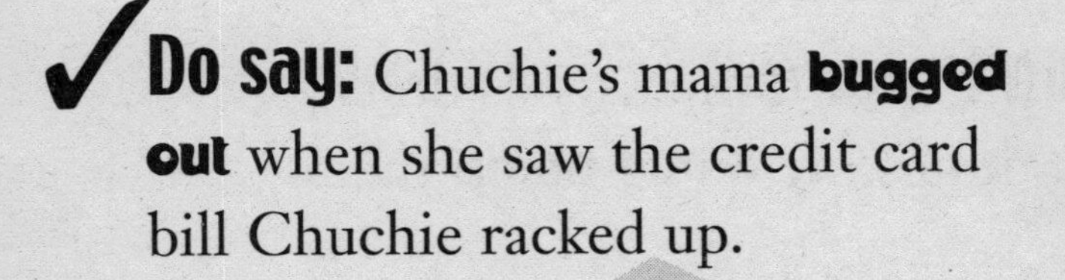

✓ **Do say:** Chuchie's mama **bugged out** when she saw the credit card bill Chuchie racked up.

✗ **Don't say:** Forget shopping, I'd rather stay home and **bug out** with my bug collection.

bump

get rid of

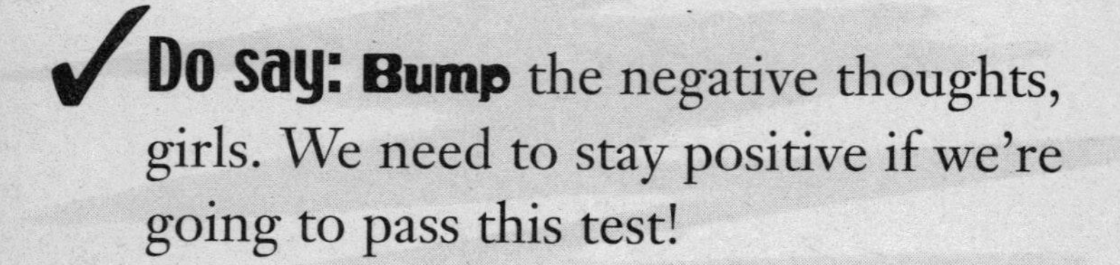

✓ **Do say:** **Bump** the negative thoughts, girls. We need to stay positive if we're going to pass this test!

✗ **Don't say:** If my friends don't do things my way, I **bump** them.

celly

cell phone

✓ **Do say:** If I'm not at home, you can catch me on my **celly**!

✗ **Don't say:** I'm going to turn off my **celly**. (Hello! Your friends might need you. Or some big agent might call to sign you. A diva *never* turns off her celly.)

The coolest of the cool. Anything can be cheetah-licious, from boys to harmonies, as long as they're the sweetest, choicest, hottest thing going.

✓ **Do say:** Chanel, that new outfit is **cheetah-licious**!

✗ **Don't say:** Ooh, we love the name Global Getdown. It's so **cheetah-licious**!

the noise we Cheetahs make when we all get together and can't stop talking

✓ **Do say:** Cut the **cheetah chatter**. We need to get down to business.

✗ **Don't say:** Don't bother to listen to the lyrics. They're just **cheetah chatter**.

Cheetah cheddar

Cash earned with our talent and skills. Cheetah cheddar is better than regular old duckets 'cause it's money we brought home ourselves.

✓ **Do say:** Let's dip into the **cheetah cheddar** and get some new microphones.

✗ **Don't say:** I've got to hit my mom up for some **cheetah cheddar** so I can go shopping.

cheetah mamas

mothers of the Cheetah Girls

✓ **Do say:** Dorothea and Juanita couldn't wait to meet Aqua's and Dó's families so they could get to know the other **cheetah mamas**!

✗ **Don't say:** Chill, **cheetah mama**, it's just one little tattoo!

the scale by which all coolness is measured

✓ **Do say:** Galleria's new lyrics just maxed out the **cheetah meter**!

✗ **Don't say:** My new sweat socks scored high points on the **cheetah meter**.

All clubs need a secret handshake for those moments of ultimate triumph, and the Cheetah Girls are no exception. Of course, the Cheetah pound isn't so secret, since we pound it often and in public, but it is all ours.

✓ **Do say:** We made the talent show? It's time for a **cheetah pound**!

✗ **Don't say:** I flunked the test. Let's have a **cheetah pound**!

crunched like corn chips

to lose or be embarrassed in a majorly public way

✓ **Do say:** If we aren't ready with our best performance, we are going to get **crunched like corn chips** at the talent show.

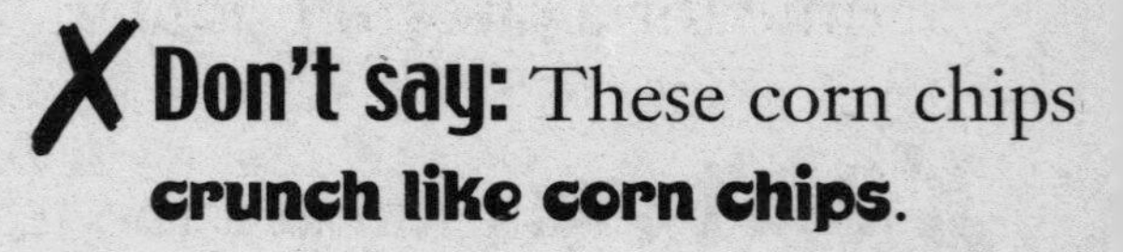

✗ **Don't say:** These corn chips **crunch like corn chips**.

to record

✓ **Do say:** We're going into the studio tomorrow to **cut** our first demo.

✗ **Don't say:** I brought the scissors. Let's go **cut** some demos!

The Down Down Low. You keep things on the DDL when they are a major secret.

✓ **Do say:** Dorinda kept her home life on the **DDL** for a while.

✗ **Don't say:** You won first prize in the talent show? Keep that on the **DDL**.

demo

a CD of sample songs

✓ **Do say:** The Cheetah Girls are going to make a **demo** and send it out to all the big radio stations!

✗ **Don't say:** Who needs a **demo** when all we do is lip-synch?

a woman who knows who she is, what she wants, and how to get it

✓ **Do say:** Drinka Champagne was one of the original **divas** of the disco era. Everyone worshipped her!

✗ **Don't say:** Who'd want to be a **diva**?

divette

a young diva

✓ **Do say:** The Cheetah Girls make those other **divettes** look like amateurs!

✗ **Don't say:** You are *so* not a **divette**, Galleria!

our hopes for the future that we can never let fade

✓ **Do say:** I'll never give up my **dreams** of winning a Grammy with the Cheetah Girls!

✗ **Don't say:** What's the point of having **dreams**?

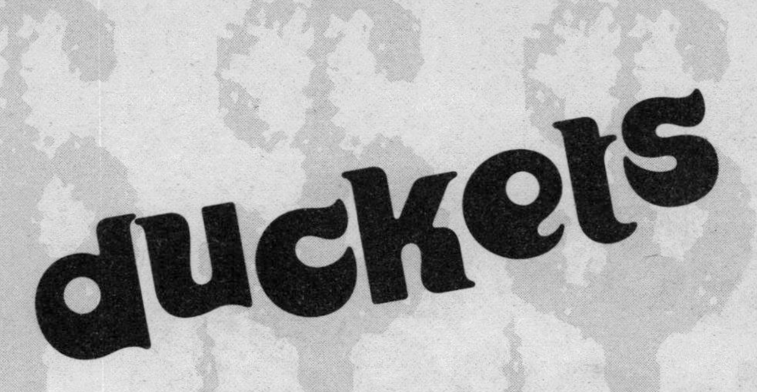

cash

✓**Do say:** Our first album is gonna make us some major **duckets**.

✗**Don't say:** I'm going to spend all my **duckets** on those trendy platform flip-flops.

effortless

✓**Do say:** That math test is not going to be **easy-breezy**. I'd better hit the books!

✗**Don't say:** Our concert tonight is going to be **easy-breezy**. We don't even need to rehearse!

when everyone knows your name (the ultimate status for a star)

✓ **Do say:** I can't wait until I'm so **famous** that all the huge designers start sending me free clothes.

✗ **Don't say:** What's so great about being **famous**?

fierce

anything cool or hot, but with extra attitude

✓ **Do say:** That high C Chanel hit was **fierce**!

✗ **Don't say:** Yum, this baloney sandwich is **fierce**.

flava

that extraspecial something that makes you stand out from the crowd

✓ **Do say:** Every time the Cheetah Girls take the stage, they prove they've got **flava**.

✗ **Don't say:** I don't like the **flava** of this ice cream.

flimflam

big fat lies

✓ **Do say:** Cut the **flimflam**, my man. We know you're not going to give us a contract unless we do it *your* way.

✗ **Don't say:** I want the straight-up **flimflam**—how's my hair look?

for real

honest and true; not kidding

✓ **Do say:** You're giving me your favorite T-shirt? Are you **for real**?

✗ **Don't say:** Sure, we'd love to be in Global Getdown. **For real**!

freak

to lose control

✓ **Do say:** My mama is going to **freak** when she finds out I forgot to give her these messages.

✗ **Don't say:** My irresponsible conduct regarding the delivery of my mother's important messages will most likely cause her to **freak**.

to go off the song sheet and sing your own melody; to make up the music as you go along, adding your own creative flava

✓ **Do say:** Aqua **freestyled** the intro to that song.

✗ **Don't say:** Want to hear me **freestyle**? I've got it all memorized!

from jump

from the beginning

✓ **Do say:** Chanel and Galleria have been best friends **from jump**.

✗ **Don't say:** I will now read my book report **from jump** to the end.

front

to cover up how you really feel; to pretend

✓ **Do say:** Don't **front**, Drinka. Tell us what you really thought of our performance.

✗ **Don't say:** When I told you I wrote those lyrics myself, I was just **frontin'**.

the mysterious line through which gossip travels

✓ **Do say:** I heard through the **grapevine** that Mackerel is going to ask Chanel to the school dance!

✗ **Don't say:** Of course it's true! I heard it through the **grapevine**.

groove

to dance

✓ **Do say:** Hit the dance floor, Dó! Let's see you **groove**!

✗ **Don't say:** Turn up the polka music so we can **groove**!

the ability to be strong and say what you mean

✓ **Do say:** We're going to need some serious **growl power** if we're going to snag a record deal.

✗ **Don't say:** Pardon me, I didn't mean to get in your face with my **growl power**.

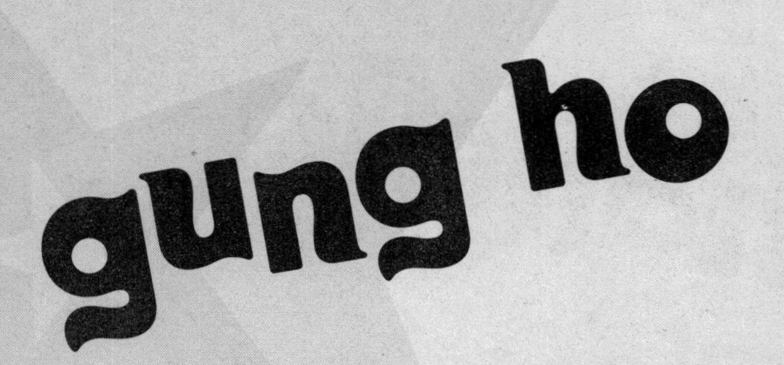

all excited and determined

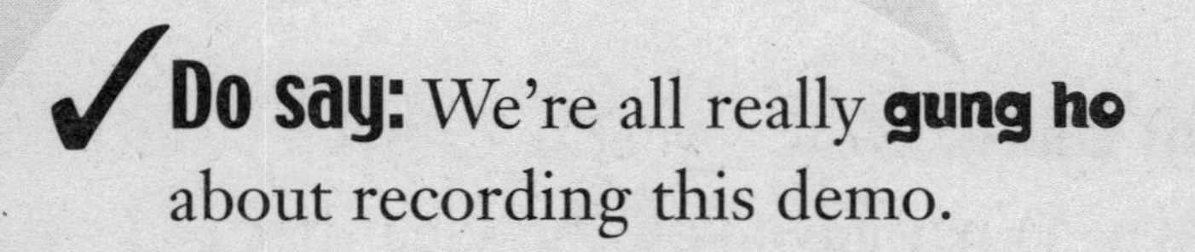

✓ **Do say:** We’re all really **gung ho** about recording this demo.

✗ **Don’t say:** We’re all really **gung ho** about detention.

to talk down to someone in an effort to calm them

✓ **Do say:** I told my mom not to **handle** me. I had a right to be upset!

✗ **Don't say:** Now, sweetie, calm down. What gave you the idea that I was trying to **handle** you?

the secondary tune of a song, usually sung by backup singers

✓ **Do say:** Dorinda and Aqua learned the **harmony** of that new song in no time!

✗ **Don't say:** **Harmony**? That's the boring stuff the backup sings, right?

harsh

extremely mean

✓ **Do say:** Aqua, what you just said to Galleria was way **harsh**. You should apologize.

✗ **Don't say:** You have to be **harsh** to get your point across.

herstory

a girl-power word for history

✓ **Do say:** Let's go over the **herstory** of ancient Greece before the test tomorrow.

✗ **Don't say:** What's the point of learning **herstory**?

high main-tenance

needing a lot of attention or spe-cial treatment

✓ **Do say:** Aqua would rather pay major duckets for a cab than ride the subway. That girl is **high maintenance**.

✗ **Don't say:** Whoa, you brush your teeth *every day*? You are *so* **high maintenance**!

hit the books

study hard

✓ **Do say:** We Cheetahs **hit the books** together before all our big exams.

✗ **Don't say:** What's the point of **hitting the books** if all I want to do in life is sing?

stop

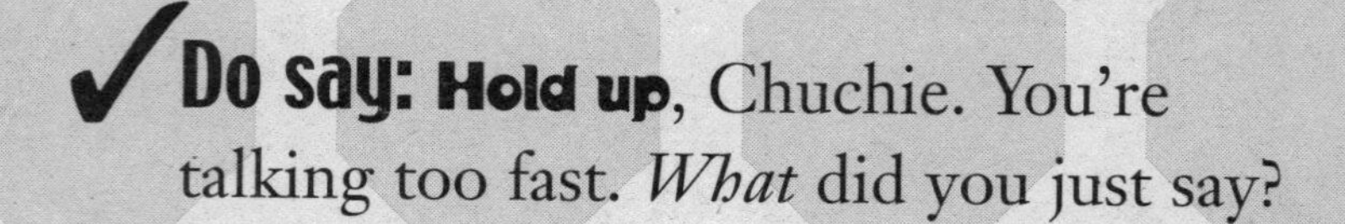

✓ **Do say:** **Hold up**, Chuchie. You're talking too fast. *What* did you just say?

✗ **Don't say:** This is a **holdup**!

diamonds

✓ **Do say:** Once we make the duckets, we're going to be dripping in **ice**.

✗ **Don't say:** I think I'm wearing too much **ice**. (Not possible!)

improvise

to make it up as you go along

✓ **Do say:** When he's at the turntables, Mackerel loves to **improvise**. You never know what he'll do next.

✗ **Don't say:** I never study for tests. I'd rather just **improvise**.

in

a connection with someone important

✓ **Do say:** We have an **in** with a producer at a major record label.

✗ **Don't say:** If you don't have an **in** with the popular crowd, you're not cool.

jam

a great song

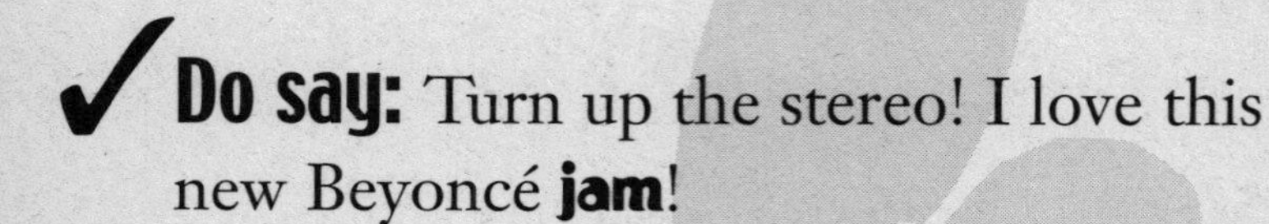

✓ **Do say:** Turn up the stereo! I love this new Beyoncé **jam**!

✗ **Don't say:** My favorite **jam** is strawberry!

jiggy jungle

the exciting, crazy, cheetah-licious world that all Cheetah Girls and the divas who came before us inhabit

✓ **Do say:** After we won the talent show, we got mad crazy up in the **jiggy jungle**.

✗ **Don't say:** You'll never see me in the **jiggy jungle**—I hate the outdoors.

Ka-ching Ka-ching

racking up the cash (comes from the sound of a cash register)

✓ **Do say:** Once our first album becomes a hit, we'll be all **Ka-ching, Ka-ching**!

✗ **Don't say:** Without the **Ka-ching Ka-ching**, we're nothing.

stay true to yourself

✓ **Do say:** The Cheetah Girls are not going to sing someone else's songs or change our name. We're **keeping it real**!

✗ **Don't say:** Global Getdown **keeps it real**. (Please!)

lip-synch

to mouth the words to a pre-recorded song

✓ **Do say:** The Cheetah Girls will never **lip-synch** in concert!

✗ **Don't say:** All my favorite performers **lip-synch**.

lite fm

unserious

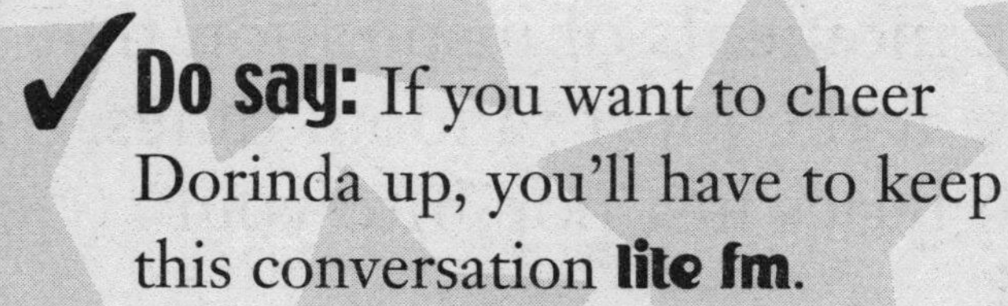

✓ **Do say:** If you want to cheer Dorinda up, you'll have to keep this conversation **lite fm**.

✗ **Don't say:** Let's turn on a **lite fm** station and groove.

lyric moment

those moments of inspiration that come at the most random times, when lyrics just pop into your head

✓ **Do say:** It's always good to keep a pen and notebook handy in case you have a **lyric moment**.

✗ **Don't say:** I usually schedule a **lyric moment** for right after lunch.

when something's not just wack, but *beyond* wack

✓ **Do say:** A pop quiz in history? That is **majordomo wack**!

✗ **Don't say:** You want to give me a record deal? That is **majordomo wack**!

makes me happy

✓ **Do say:** That Aqua has so many quirks, she just **makes me giggle**.

✗ **Don't say:** When someone stubs their toe, it **makes me giggle**.

the primary tune of a song, usually sung by the lead singer

✓ **Do say:** Galleria, I love the **melody** you wrote for our new song.

✗ **Don't say:** Let's have Pucci write the **melody** for our next ballad.

huge

✓ **Do say:** Ashanti's new song is a **monster** hit!

✗ **Don't say:** (to your friend) You wear size *ten* shoes? Whoa, girl, you've got **monster** feet!

my bad

my mistake

✓ **Do say:** Sorry I missed the intro on that song. **My bad**.

✗ **Don't say:** Sorry I spent all the Cheetah cheddar from our last gig on candy bars. **My bad**!

my girl

my best friend

✓ **Do say:** Chuchie, no matter what happens, you will always be **my girl**.

✗ **Don't say:** What do you mean you're hanging out with some other friends? You're ***my* girl**!

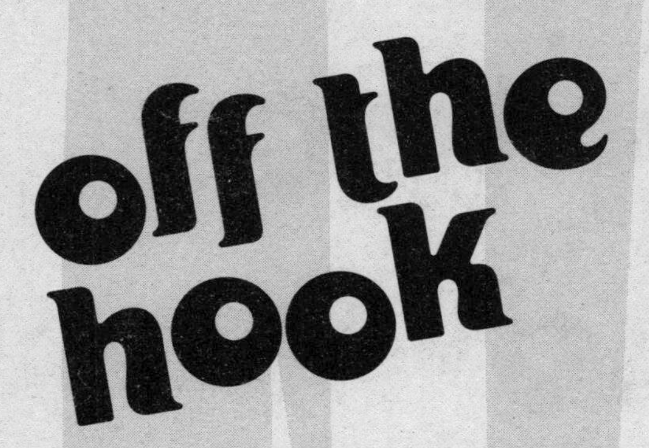

coolest, hottest, craziest fun

✓ **Do say:** That Cheetah Girls concert was **off the hook**!

✗ **Don't say:** The school spelling bee was **off the hook**.

on the move

doing what it takes to be successful

✓ **Do say:** With their new hit single and number one video, the Cheetah Girls are **on the move**!

✗ **Don't say:** Check out my new roller skates. I'm **on the move**!

one hundred and ten percent

better than the best

✓ **Do say:** When it comes to performing, the Cheetah Girls always give **one hundred and ten percent**.

✗ **Don't say:** I am just too tired to give **one hundred and ten percent** at the talent show.

too much

✓ **Do say:** Galleria, don't you think the cat's-eye sunglasses with the full Cheetah-print catsuit are a little bit **over the top**?

✗ **Don't say:** (to your teacher) You want me to come to class on time *with* my homework finished? That is *so* **over the top**!

playin'

messing around or lying

✓ **Do say:** We won the lottery, Papa? You better not be **playin'**.

✗ **Don't say:** We're **playin'** chess after school today.

pounce to the ounce

talent

✓ **Do say:** The Cheetah Girls have so much **pounce to the ounce**, their new single is sure to be a monster hit!

✗ **Don't say:** Galleria has no **pounce to the ounce**.

props

compliments or credit

✓ **Do say:** I want to give **props** to all the other competitors in the talent show.

✗ **Don't say:** **Props** to the chef who made the peanut-butter-and-pickle sandwiches.

Psych

just kidding

✓ **Do say:** I've decided to go solo. . . . **Psych**! You know I would never leave the Cheetahs.

✗ **Don't say:** You're the best singer I ever heard! **Psych**!

quarter past time to be on time

way late

✓ **Do say:** We were supposed to start rehearsal fifteen minutes ago! Girl, you are **quarter past time to be on time**.

✗ **Don't say:** You are **quarter past time to be on time**. We've been waiting on you forever!

raggedy

torn, frayed, or just plain old

✓**Do say:** I need a new jacket. This one is all **raggedy**.

✗**Don't say:** Dorinda, why don't you get rid of those **raggedy** clothes you always wear?

so beautiful and elegant it could be worn for the paparazzi and all the world to see

✓ **Do say:** Mama, that new gown you made for Juanita is totally **red carpet-worthy**.

✗ **Don't say:** Check out my flannel pajamas. **Red carpet-worthy**, right?

seal the deal

do what it takes to accomplish something big

✓ **Do say:** All we have to do is write one more hit and that will **seal the deal** with the record company.

✗ **Don't say:** I would sell my soul to **seal the deal**.

shimmer

shiny accessories or makeup that make you look like a star

✓ **Do say:** Just add a little **shimmer** to that costume and you'll look like a true diva.

✗ **Don't say:** I don't think we need any **shimmer** onstage.

shoe-shoppy

that feeling you get when you just *need* to drop some major duckets on some spankin' new kicks

✓ **Do say:** Let's hit the stores! I'm feeling **shoe-shoppy**!

✗ **Don't say:** I finally wore out my old sneakers. Guess I'd better get **shoe-shoppy**.

shout-out

a way to call attention and give props to your friends

✓ **Do say:** I'd like to give a **shout-out** to all the kids at Manhattan Magnet School!

✗ **Don't say:** A big **shout-out** to the kid who came to school sick and gave us all chicken pox!

skills

superspecial talents

Do say: Have you seen Mackerel on stage? That boy has got **skills**!

✗ Don't say: Some people just don't have **skills**. (Everybody's good at something!)

so fine

totally gorgeous, charming, and cool

✓ **Do say:** I adore Derek. He is just **so fine**!

✗ **Don't say:** I adore my pet rat. He is just **so fine**!

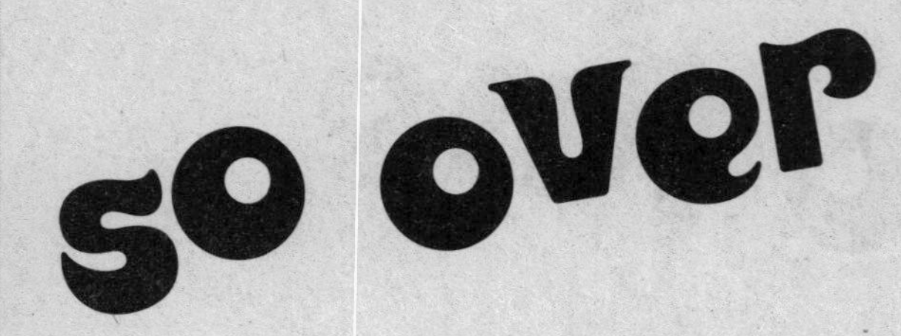

done

✓ **Do say:** The grunge look is **so over**.

✗ **Don't say:** I am **so over** being a Cheetah!

solo

alone

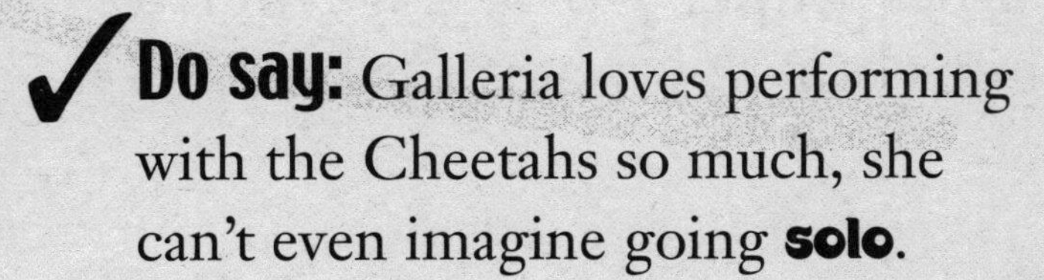

✓ **Do say:** Galleria loves performing with the Cheetahs so much, she can't even imagine going **solo**.

✗ **Don't say:** You want to take me to the school dance, Derek? No thanks, I'd rather go **solo**.

spectaculous

used to describe something so amazing, you have to squash two super-duper words together to get your point across

✓ **Do say:** The new costumes Dorothea made for us are absolutely **spectaculous**!

✗ **Don't say:** Barcelona is a **spectaculous** town.

squash the drama

stop being so dramatic

✓ **Do say: Squash the drama**, Derek. It's just one bad haircut!

✗ **Don't say: Squash the drama**, Toto. I'll walk you in an hour.

stay true

Be yourself and don't let anything (like success, fame, or fortune) change you.

✓ **Do say:** Even if the Cheetah Girls become the biggest group in the world, we will always **stay true**.

✗ **Don't say:** What's the point in **staying true** if you're not making mad cash?

to be really, *really* lousy

✓ **Do say:** Have you seen Bobby's mime act? It **stinks like cheap cologne**.

✗ **Don't say:** (to your dad) Papa, your new cologne **stinks like cheap cologne**.

technical difficulties

problems with the stage, lights, or sound system that affect the performance

✓ **Do say:** The show was great, except for that small **technical difficulty** when the microphones stopped working.

✗ **Don't say:** If we have even one **technical difficulty,** I am walking off the stage. (Hey, the show must go on!)

totally cool

✓**Do say:** That new harmony is **tight**!

✗**Don't say:** Drinka, your dress is **tight**. (That could be taken the wrong way!)

torn up

mismatched, messy, or just out of style

✓ **Do say:** Dorinda freaked when Galleria said she looked **torn up**.

✗ **Don't say:** Dorinda, you look **torn up**.

touring

taking the band on the road to several different cities and venues

✓ **Do say:** If Dorinda takes the Gold Medal Crew's offer, she'll be **touring** with them all over the United States this summer.

✗ **Don't say:** I'd rather hang out at the beach this summer than go **touring** with the Cheetah Girls.

track

one song on an album

✓ **Do say:** The first **track** on the Cheetah Girls album is going to be tight!

✗ **Don't say:** You want me to check out a new **track**? Great! I love running.

trippin'

acting or thinking crazy

✓ **Do say:** You want the Cheetah Girls to lip-synch? You must be **trippin'**.

✗ **Don't say:** You're going to give us free manicures and pedicures? You must be **trippin'**!

turn up the heat

take it to the next level

✓ **Do say:** Let's **turn up the heat** in these dance moves.

✗ **Don't say:** Can you **turn up the heat**? I'm cold!

wack-attack

a total meltdown

✓ **Do say:** If Aqua has to get on the subway again, she is going to have a serious **wack-attack**.

✗ **Don't say:** I'm having a bad hair day. Time for a **wack-attack**.

to leave someone or something behind

✓ **Do say:** If Jackal Johnson tries to make us change our name, Galleria is going to **walk**.

✗ **Don't say:** If that fine guy smiles at me one more time, I'm going to **walk**.

any smart move

✓**Do say:** I'll do **whatever's clever** to help the Cheetah Girls succeed.

✗**Don't say:** I'll do **whatever's clever** to cheat on the test.

work it

show some serious moves on the dance floor

✓ **Do say:** Did you see the new Usher video? He was **working it**.

✗ **Don't say:** We want to see the lunch ladies get out there and **work it**.

what's in a name?

Every name has a meaning behind it. Some people even think that when our parents give us a name, they're determining our destiny. Check out the meaning of the Cheetah Girls' names. Think they relate to our personalities?

galleria: Mama says she named me after the Galleria, a superhuge mall in Dallas, Texas, that's full of colorful, amazing, beautiful things. Just like me! (Aw! Isn't she sweet?)

chanel: Coco Chanel was an incredible, sophisticated fashion designer who also created the most famous perfume in the world, Chanel No. 5. (The perfect name for our fashion-obsessed Chanel, no?)

aqua: Blue-green, like the color of the Caribbean Sea.

dorinda: Talented. (You got that right!)

pucci: A famous fashion designer from the 1960s. His work was wild and colorful (kind of like our little Pucci!).

dorothea: Gift of God. (That definitely fits my mama!)

francobollo: In Italian, *francobollo* means "postage stamp." (What were my grandparents *thinking*?)

jackal: A wild dog, kind of like a coyote. Jackals are known for being clever and wily. (Sound like any producers you know?)

derek: Famous ruler. (No wonder he has such an ego!)

mackerel: A fish of the north Atlantic Ocean, with blue, green, and silver scales. (I don't even know what to say about that! Does Chanel know she's crushing on a *fish*?)

new york lingo

You know that old saying about New York, "If you can make it there, you can make it anywhere"? Well, here are a few words you need to know to survive in the big city.

broadway: Neon lights, huge theaters, dance schools, comedy clubs. If something's happening in New York, there's a good chance it's happening on Broadway.

day spa: Where the divas go to get facials, manicures, pedicures, and massages, among other things. Dorothea and Juanita are VIPs at some of the best day spas in town.

fifth avenue: Every chic designer in the world has a boutique on Fifth Avenue. For primo window-shopping, this is the place to be.

manhattan: Sometimes called the Big Apple—or Manny Hanny if you're a Cheetah Girl—Manhattan is at the center of New York's five boroughs. It is home to all the swankiest restaurants, theaters, and shops—not to mention the school of cool, Manhattan Magnet. The four surrounding boroughs are Brooklyn, Queens, the Bronx, and Staten Island.

penthouse: The penthouse apartment is on the top floor of an apartment building and is the nicest pad in the place. Once the Cheetah Girls hit the big time, we're definitely snagging a penthouse.

street smarts: There's book smarts and then there's street smarts. Book smarts might get you into college, but street smarts will get you around the city. Being street smart involves knowing which subways and buses will take you where you want to go, mastering the two-fingered whistle (see next page), knowing how to stretch your allowance, and carrying yourself with confidence so no one will mess with you. Chanel is our current queen of street smarts.

subway: This underground train will take you anywhere you want to go in Manhattan, Brooklyn, Queens, and the Bronx. That is, if you can figure out the system and don't mind the grime.

two-fingered whistle:
The whistle for getting a cab to stop.

fabulous fashion speak

Being a superstar isn't just about talent. You've got to maintain an image, and that means being up on all the latest styles. Here are just a few words every fashionista should know. (BTW, a fashionista is a person who is obsessed with fashion!)

boa: A true diva accessory, a boa is a long feather or fur scarf.

cabbie: A cool flat hat with a short front brim. This is one of Dó's favorite accessories.

choker: A supershort necklace that clings to your neck.

couture: The absolute highest fashion; the best the designers have to offer. You need to have major duckets to afford couture.

cubic zirconium: The finest in fake ice. Only a jeweler can tell the difference.

fashion week: One week in the fall, and another in the spring, when designers, models, photographers, and celebs descend on New York City to present fashion shows, throw parties, and snag major photo ops. Basically the coolest two weeks of the year.

faux fur: Fake furs are much better than the real thing. Not only do you spare an innocent animal's life, but they come in hundreds of fierce colors!

kicks: Comfy sneakers.

leg warmers: Like long socks without feet, leg warmers come in all kinds of colors and patterns.

petticoat: A ruffled underskirt that makes your skirt flounce out. Definitely an Aqua fave.

poncho: A round, blanketlike sweater without sleeves. A very comfy, yet stylish, solution for those cold New York City nights.

sample sale: Monster retail event where designers mark down their stuff. No self-respecting diva misses one.

spree: One of those mall trips where you spend, spend, spend! (And explain later.)

stilts: High heels. You should always carry your stilts in your bag and wear your kicks, just in case you have to walk farther than expected. Stilts look good, but they can be a real pain in the foot!

a cheetah tale

Once you've studied up on your Cheetah lingo, play this little game with your friends to see how much you know! One person, the reader, holds the book. (You'll need a pencil, too!) The reader then asks the other players to help her fill in the blanks. Have your friends give you a verb for each verb space, a noun for each noun space, and so on. Fill in each word as you go, and at the end, read the story aloud to your friends. The results will be hilarious! (Note: Don't tell your friends what the story is about. It makes the results even funnier!)

the missing boa

Galleria ________________ backstage,
ACTION VERB + "ED"
looking panicked.

"Chuchie? Have you seen my __________
ADJECTIVE
new boa?" she asked.

Chanel puckered her lips and finished applying her ____________ in the mirror.
NOUN
"No. Where was the last place you had it?"

Galleria threw up her ____________ . "I
BODY PART
swear I put it in my ______________ bag." She
ADJECTIVE
picked up the bag and dug through it. "It's not here!"

"Hey, girls!" Dorinda called out, walking in and _____________ her own boa around her
VERB + "ING"
neck. "We're on in five minutes! Everybody ready?"

"No! I can't find my ____________
NOUN

," Galleria cried. "Oh, Mama is going to ____________ (VERB). That boa is worth some serious____________ (NOUN)."

"What's the problem here, Cheetahs?" Aqua asked, joining them.

"Bubbles is ____________ (VERB + "ING") 'cause she lost her boa," Chanel said.

"And I can't go on without it," Galleria added. "If you guys all have yours and I don't have mine, we're gonna look all ____________ (ADJECTIVE)."

"Okay, everybody ____________ (VERB)," Aqua said. "Let's spread out and search the area."

The four girls split up. Galleria looked through the dressing room, but all she found were a bunch of ____________ (ADJECTIVE) ____________ (PLURAL NOUN). Chanel checked with the sound engineer, but he was so ____________ (ADJECTIVE) she forgot why she was there. Dorinda peeked through the stage curtains, but then she saw the huge audience and

__________ . Galleria was starting to
VERB + "ED"
think she would never see her __________
ADJECTIVE
boa again.

"Galleria!" Aqua called out. "I think I found something you should see."

Galleria, Chanel, and Dorinda all came running. They cracked up laughing when they saw what Aqua had found.

Toto, Galleria's __________ , was
ANIMAL
curled up in the corner on top of a
__________ boa.
ADJECTIVE

"He must have stolen it from your
__________ !" Dorinda said.
NOUN

"At least we know he has __________
ADJECTIVE
taste!" Chanel joked.

"That's my little Cheetah puppy," she cooed. "You definitely know fine
__________ when you see it!"
NOUN

in case of emergency...

Last but not least, we want to share some of our favorite phrases for those crucial moments in life.

top five ways to blow off a guy

"You are so not worthy."

Because, really, what guy *is* worthy of your fabulousness?

"basta pasta"

Basically this means "enough already." But he probably won't know that, so he'll just walk away confused. Mission accomplished!

"Talk to the hand."

When accompanied by a firm, flat, raised hand, no one has a comeback for this one.

"Keep dreaming, baby. If you don't have your dreams, you don't have anything."

This is our favorite. It's just so diva-worthy.

"Latah, hatah."

Basic, but it gets the job done!

top five ways to cheer up a girlfriend when she's down

"You are looking fierce!"
Everyone knows that if you look good, you feel good. So tell a mamacita when she's turning heads.

"With that voice, you could give Mary J. a run for her money."
If she's down on her skills, this is the best compliment you can give.

"Girl, your moves got sugar and spice and everything nice."
Looking supersweet on the dance floor is always a major mood-lifter.

"You're my girl."
What better way to cheer up a friend than to remind her of how much she means to you!

"You are a true diva, and you've got the growl power of all the cheetah-licious divas who came before you to keep you strong."
A Cheetah-power pep talk always works wonders on the spirit.

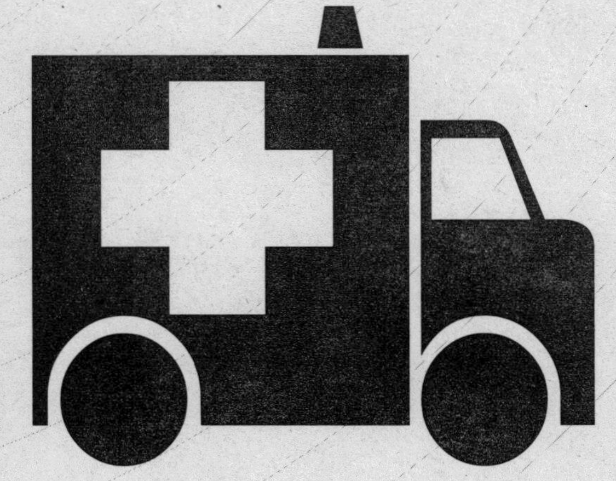